Willie's Birthday

Story by **Anastasia Suen**

Illustrations by **Allan Eitzen**

Based on the characters created by
Ezra Jack Keats

PUFFIN BOOKS

PUFFIN BOOKS
Published by the Penguin Group
Penguin Putnam Books for Young Readers, 345 Hudson Street, New York, New York 10014, U.S.A.
Penguin Books Ltd, 80 Strand, London WC2R ORL, England
Penguin Books Australia Ltd, Ringwood, Victoria, Australia
Penguin Books Canada Ltd, 10 Alcorn Avenue, Toronto, Ontario, Canada M4V 3B2
Penguin Books (N.Z.) Ltd, 182-190 Wairau Road, Auckland 10, New Zealand

Penguin Books Ltd, Registered Offices: Harmondsworth, Middlesex, England

First published in the United States of America by Viking,
a division of Penguin Putnam Books for Young Readers, 2001
Published by Puffin Books, a division of Penguin Putnam Books for Young Readers, 2002

1 3 5 7 9 10 8 6 4 2

Copyright © Ezra Jack Keats Foundation, 2001
All rights reserved
Text by Anastasia Suen
Illustrations by Allan Eitzen

THE LIBRARY OF CONGRESS HAS CATALOGED THE VIKING EDITION AS FOLLOWS:
Suen, Anastasia.
Willie's birthday / by Anastasia Suen ; illustrations by Allan Eitzen ;
based on characters of Ezra Jack Keats.
p. cm.
Summary: A "Bring Your Pet" birthday party gets out of hand when
the pets show more interest in chasing each other than in celebrating.
ISBN 0-670-88943-1
[1. Dogs—Fiction. 2. Pets—Fiction. 3. Birthdays—Fiction.]
I. Eitzen, Allan, ill. II. Keats, Ezra Jack. III. Title.
PZ7.S94343 Wi 2001 [E]—dc21 00-009734

Puffin Easy-to-Read ISBN 0-14-230135-3
Puffin® and Easy-to-Read® are registered trademarks of Penguin Putnam Inc.

Printed in Hong Kong

Except in the United States of America, this book is sold subject to the condition that it shall not,
by way of trade or otherwise, be lent, re-sold, hired out, or otherwise circulated without the publisher's
prior consent in any form of binding or cover other than that in which it is published and without
a similar condition including this condition being imposed on the subsequent purchaser.

Reading Level 1.8

Willie's Birthday

It was Willie's birthday.

He sat and stared at the door.

"When will the party start?" asked Susie.

"As soon as everyone gets here," said Peter.

He put the birthday cake on the table.

Ding dong!

Arf! Arf! barked Willie.

"Hooray!" said Susie. "They're here!"

"Are you ready, birthday boy?"

asked Peter.

"Happy birthday, Willie," said Archie.

"Happy birthday, Willie," said Amy.

Willie wagged his tail at them.

"This is for you, Willie," said Archie.

He put a present on the floor.

"Here's another one, Willie," said Amy.

Willie sniffed the presents.

He pulled on the ribbon.

"Not yet!" said Peter.

Peter put the presents on the table.

Arf! Arf! barked Willie.

He ran in circles around the table.

Meow! went Archie's cat.

She jumped on the couch.

Yoo hoo! said Amy's parrot.

It flew off Amy's shoulder

and flew over the couch.

Arf! Arf! barked Willie.

Meow! went the cat.

Yoo hoo! said the parrot.

"Come here, silly Willie," said Peter.

"Yes," said Susie, "it's time for party hats."

She gave Peter, Archie, and Amy a hat.

"Can your cat wear a hat?" asked Susie.

"I don't know," said Archie, "but we can try.

"I'll hold the cat, you put on the hat," he said.

"Hooray!" said Susie.

She put the hat on the cat, but . . .

Meow!

The cat hit the hat with her paw.

She jumped out of Archie's arms.

Yoo hoo!

Amy's parrot flew down and picked

up the hat.

Then the parrot flew away.

Arf! Arf!

Willie ran after the parrot.

The cat jumped onto the table.

Water sloshed out of the fishbowl.

Meow! purred the cat.

"My fish!" said Susie. "Shoo! Go away!"

Archie took the cat off the table.

"It's not time to eat," said Archie.

Amy whistled.

The parrot flew back and

landed on her shoulder.

"Come here, silly Willie," said Peter.

"Let's play a game."

"What kind of game?" asked Archie.

"Pin the tail on the dog?"

Arf! Arf!

"No one will pin you, Willie," said Peter.

"He already has a tail," said Susie. "See?"

"So what is the game?" asked Archie.

"Give the dog a bone," said Peter.

"A *paper* bone," said Susie.

Everyone laughed.

"Can I put the blindfold on Willie?"

 asked Susie.

"Okay," said Peter.

 Willie licked Peter's face.

"Hold still, silly Willie," said Peter.

"I can't tie it," said Susie.

"Let me help," said Amy.

Yoo hoo!

Amy's parrot flew off her shoulder.

Arf! Arf!

Willie wiggled and barked at the parrot.

The cat hissed and jumped on the table.

Meow! purred the cat.

She put her paw into the fishbowl.

"My fish!" said Susie.

She let go of the blindfold.

"Shoo! Shoo! Go away!"

Willie jumped out of Peter's arms.

Arf! Arf! he barked.

Meow! went the cat.

Peter picked up the fishbowl.

"Safe!" he said.

Willie grabbed the tablecloth, and pulled.

The cat jumped off the table . . .

and the cake fell on the floor.

"Willie!" said Peter.

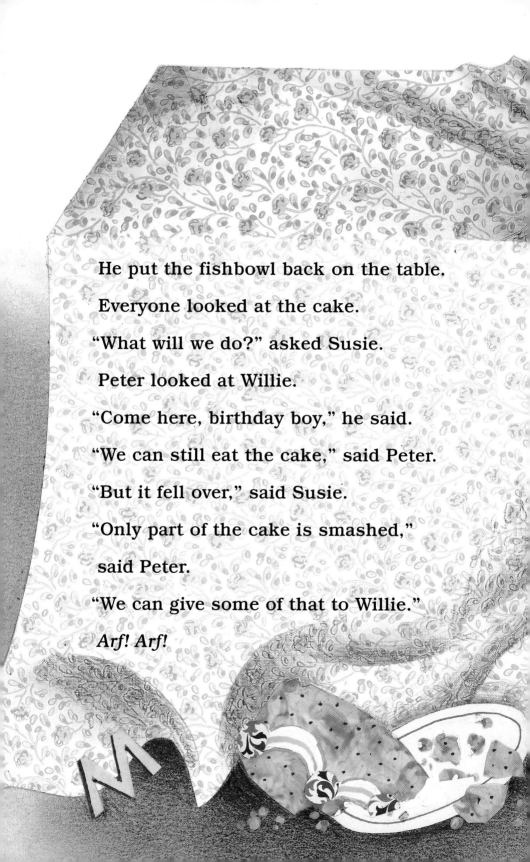

He put the fishbowl back on the table.

Everyone looked at the cake.

"What will we do?" asked Susie.

Peter looked at Willie.

"Come here, birthday boy," he said.

"We can still eat the cake," said Peter.

"But it fell over," said Susie.

"Only part of the cake is smashed,"

said Peter.

"We can give some of that to Willie."

Arf! Arf!

Everyone laughed.

Peter cut the cake.

He gave Willie the first piece.

"Happy birthday, silly Willie!"